THE WIND IN THE WILLOWS

by KENNETH GRAHAME

#2 The Open Road

Adapted by Laura Driscoll

Illustrated by Ann Iosa

Spotlight

Sterling Publishing Co., Inc.
New York

visit us at www.abdopublishing.com

Reinforced library bound edition published in 2008 by Spotlight, a division of the ABDO Publishing Group, 8000 West 78th Street, Edina, Minnesota 55439. Published by agreement with Sterling Publishing Co., Inc.

Originally published and © 2003 by Barnes and Noble, Inc.
Illustrations © 2003 by Ann Iosa
Cover illustration by Ann Iosa

Library of Congress Cataloging-in-Publication Data
This title was previously cataloged with the following information:

Driscoll, Laura.
    The wind in the willows. #2, The open road / by Kenneth Grahame ; adapted by Laura Driscoll ; illustrated by Ann Iosa.
        p. cm. -- (Easy reader classics)
    Summary: A brief, simplified retelling of the episode in "The Wind in the Willows" during which Rat takes Mole to meet Mr. Toad and together they set off on a road trip in Toad's colorful new cart.
    [1. Animals--Fiction. 2. Voyages and Travels--Fiction.] I. Iosa, Ann, ill. II. Grahame, Kenneth, 1859-1932. III. Title.
PZ7.D79 Ope 2006
[E]--dc22   2005026589

ISBN 978-1-59961-341-3 (reinforced library bound edition)

Contents

A Visit
4

Mr. Toad
11

On the Road
17

Beep! Beep!
23

A Visit

Mole was so happy.
His friend Rat was taking
him to see Mr. Toad!
Mole had heard a lot
about Toad.
Mole knew that Toad
lived in a big house.
He knew that Toad
liked new things.

One time,
Mole had even seen Toad.
Toad had sailed by
in his new boat, but
Mole had never met Toad.

"It is never a bad time
to visit Toad!" said Rat.
So off they went
up the river.
Soon they came
around a bend and . . .

"There's Toad Hall!"
said Rat.
He pointed at
a huge brick house.
"Toad is very rich,
you know," Rat said.

Mole and Rat
landed their boat
in Toad's boathouse.
There they saw
Toad's fancy boats.
It looked like they
had not been used
in a long time.

"Toad must be tired
of boats,"
Rat said to Mole.
"I wonder what new thing
he likes now?"

Mr. Toad

Mole and Rat walked
toward Toad Hall.
They found Toad
sitting on the lawn.
"Hooray!" cried Toad
when he saw Rat and Mole.

Toad jumped up.
"It is so lucky you
came by!" Toad said.

Toad was planning a trip.

But it was not a boat trip.

Rat was right—

Toad was tired of boats.

"I have found a new way
to travel!" said Toad.
He showed Mole and Rat
his brand-new cart.
It was yellow and green,
with red wheels.

And that was just the outside!
Inside there were
beds to sleep in,
a table,
and a stove.
There were pots and pans,
lots of food,
and even a bird
in a birdcage!

Toad was planning
a road trip in his cart.
He wanted Rat and Mole to
come with him!

On the Road

Rat did not want to go.
"I am going to stick
to my old river," said Rat.
Mole was going
to stick with Rat.
"But it *does* sound
like fun," said Mole.
He sounded a little sad.

Mole *did* want to go
on the trip.
Rat could tell.
So Rat gave in.

After lunch,
Toad, Rat, and Mole
set off on the road.

They traveled all day.

The sun was warm.

The air was fresh.

At night,

they camped in a field.

They ate dinner

under the stars.

Then they went to sleep

in their beds.

The next day
was the same.
They traveled all day.

They camped at night.

Beep! Beep!

On the third day,
they were walking
down the road.
They heard a noise
behind them.
First it was a soft hum.
Then it was
a loud *beep-beep*!

In a flash,
a car whizzed by them.
Mole, Rat, and Toad
had to jump
out of the way.

The horse reared and . . .

crash!

The cart fell into a ditch.

"You road hog!"
shouted Rat.
He shook his fist at the car
as it sped away.

Toad just sat down
in the road and stared
as the car drove away.
"Beep-beep! Beep-beep!"
he said, smiling.
Toad really liked the
sound the car horn made.
"Beep-beep! Beep-beep!"

"Do not worry,"
Rat said to Toad.
"The cart can be fixed."
But Toad said,
"Fix the cart?
I never want
to see the cart again!"

Mole and Rat
could not believe it!
Toad was already
tired of carts.
He had just seen
something newer.
For Toad,
that meant something *better.*

The road trip was over.
So Rat, Mole, and Toad
made their way home.

And do you know
what silly Toad bought
the very next day?

Beep-beep! Beep-beep!